# Tales from the Manger

Written by Chonda and David Pierce
Illustrated by Matt LeBarre

Zonderkidz

Zonder**kidz**®
*The children's group of Zondervan*

www.zonderkidz.com

*Tales from the Manger*


Requests for information should be addressed to:
Zonderkidz, Grand Rapids, Michigan 49530

---

**Library of Congress Cataloging-in-Publication Data**
Pierce, Chonda.
Tales from the manger / by Chonda and David Pierce ; illustrated by Matt Le Barre. – 1st ed.
p. cm.
Summary: A collection of animals is unhappy when a man with a lamp enters their stable one night with his wife, but when her baby is born they realize they are looking upon the son of God, who made them all.
ISBN 0-310-70849-4 (softcover)
[1. Domestic animals—Fiction. 2. Animals—Fiction. 3. Conduct of life—Fiction. 4. Jesus Christ—Nativity—Fiction.] I. Pierce, David. II. Le Barre, Matt, ill. III. Title.

PZ7.P61173Tal 2004
[Fic]--dc22

2004000191

---



*Editor: Gwen Ellis*
*Art Direction: Laura M. Maitner*

*Printed in China*

---

04 05 06 07/HK/ 4 3 2 1

To all the children at World Outreach Church
in Murfreesboro—fast, slow, loud, quiet, tall and short,
who like to climb in trees or sit and read—Merry Christmas!
Chonda and David Pierce

To my daughter,
Camille Isabella LeBarre
MJL

# Contents

# Introduction

Long ago, in a little town called Bethlehem, a man stepped into a small stable and set a clay lamp on a shelf above a manger. Then he left. He returned a few moments later with his young wife. That's when the miracle happened. The light in the stable grew brighter. The man and the woman and the animals celebrated. And the whole world heard about what happened in their stable that night.

## One

# Mary and Martha Mouse

Two mice scurried from the shadows and stepped into the ring of yellow light from the lamp. They were the first to see . . . the first to know . . . and they ran to tell everyone.

"Wow!" Mary the Mouse said to her sister, as she stared at the manger. "I've never seen anything like this!"

"Me either," said her sister, Martha.

"We should have a party," said Mary.

"A party?" said Martha. "Sure, but first we should tidy

up. The stable floor is messy—all that straw and hay. And we'll need invitations and decorations and maybe some fruit punch–"

"Forget the fruit punch," Mary interrupted. "Let's invite everyone right now. They can come as they are." She scampered off.

Martha started to tidy up, but it was too much. Soon she gave up and hurried off after her sister. Together they scurried up and scurried down, scurried right and scurried left.

They scurried all over the little stable to announce this very special party.

“I’ll handle the big guy—the ox,” said Martha. “I know how to deal with bullies.”

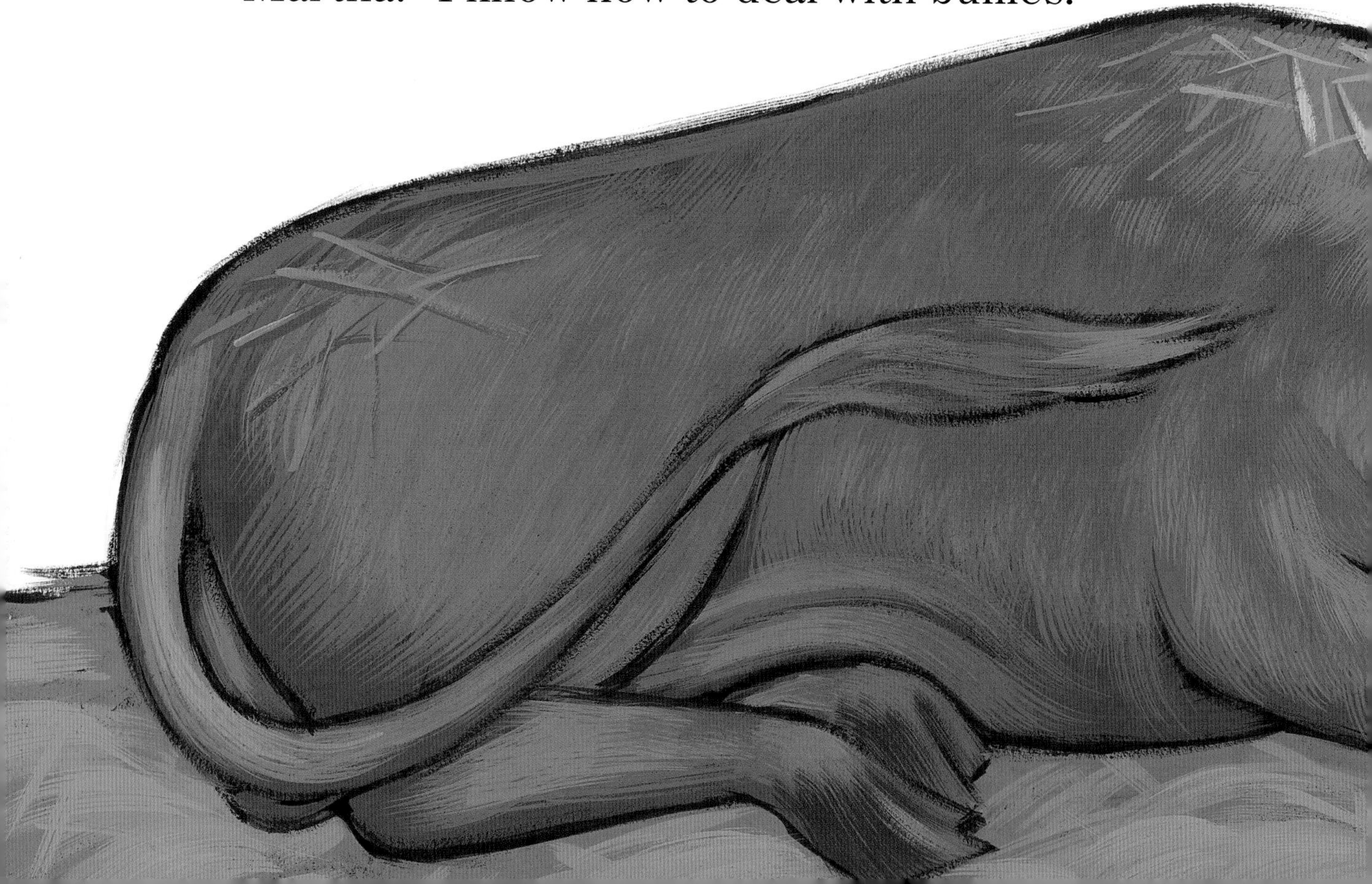

She scampered up onto a pile of hay right in front of the ox and said in a squeaky voice, "We're having a party—you're invited."

The ox bellowed, "Get out of here and stop walking on my dinner!" So Martha

leaped off the hay
and ran away.
Mary asked
the sheep if he
would come to the party.
He thought about it for a
moment, but instead
of answering, he just
started singing,
"Baaaaaa! Baaaaaa!"

Mary covered her ears and ran away.

Moments later, Mary and Martha asked the rooster if he would come to the party. He tucked his head under one wing and without peeking said in a muffled voice, “I doubt it. You see, I’ve quit being a rooster. So go wake yourself up in the morning because I’ll be sleeping.”

They tried to ask the opossum, but he was playing dead, so they couldn't invite him.

They approached a cat curled up in a corner. "We're having a party," they said to the cat. But all the cat could say was, "Meow!"

What were they going to do? How could they convince everyone that something humongous had happened right there in that smelly little stable and it was a time to celebrate?

Just then, the baby—the one Mary and Martha were trying to tell everyone about—

cried. It was a long, loud cry that made all the animals hush. From that moment on, everything changed. The ox, the sheep, the opossum, the cat, and the mice all changed. Why, even that old rooster found a new reason to crow.

It was a new beginning ...

## TWO

# Saul the Ox

The little stable had been dark for a long, long time. But now with the clay lamp giving off its bright light, the sheep could see the chickens, the mice could see the opossum, and the donkey could see the ox. Light was a big change for the animals—except for the ox.

It would take more than light to change that big old wrinkled bully.

And was Saul the Ox ever a bully! No matter where the sheep went, the ox always said, “Move over! You’re in my way!”

And whenever the owl would sing, "Who? Who?" from above, the ox would say, "You know who. Be quiet, I'm trying to sleep!"

And whenever a tiny mouse would nibble on just a single piece of hay, the ox would shout, "Stop eating all my hay!"

All Saul the Ox wanted was peace and quiet and hay—lots of hay.

No one wanted to be near the big bully ox, but it wasn't easy to get away from him in the small stable. And now that the light lit up the whole room, the ox wasn't happy staying in his own spot. He wanted everyone else's spot!

"Outta my way!" he told the chickens. "This looks like a good place for me." The chickens clucked and scattered as the ox moved into their spot.

"Scoot over, donkey," he said. "Can't you see I'm trying to stand here?" And the donkey had to find a new spot.

"If you don't
get out of my
way," said the ox
to the opossum,
"you'll be
playing dead
for good!" And
the opossum
jumped to his
feet and scurried

up a wooden post so he wouldn't be squashed.

"Who? Who?" sang the startled owl.

"Quiet up there!" growled the ox, his mouth full of hay. He was such a bully, and he had no manners whatsoever.

He also had no friends. So he stood there alone—right where the chickens, the donkey, and the opossum used to be. He ate his hay slowly and chewed his cud over and over.

He dared anyone (especially that baaaad sheep) to make him budge.

## Three

# Peter the Sheep

Peter the Sheep wasn't mean, at least not on purpose, like the ox. But everyone knew Peter was bad—not mean, just bad. "Peter?" they'd say. "Yeah, he's bad. He's real baaaaaad."

Peter hadn't started out being bad. You see, sheep are good at only two things: growing wool and following. And it so happened that Peter was very good at both.

If there had ever been a wool-growing contest held in Bethlehem, Peter would have won it. He could grow wool better than any other sheep.

And could he ever follow! The shepherd would turn left—Peter would turn left.

The shepherd would turn right—he'd turn right. But somewhere along the way Peter started following the wrong crowd. He was led astray. And since he was a really good follower, he became really bad, really fast.

When a sheep goes bad, he begins to do all sorts of things to annoy other sheep—like resting while the others are trying to move along to find grass to eat. Or pretending to be a wolf and scaring everyone. Or singing when everyone else is trying to sleep.

This night, when the man walked in and set the lamp on the shelf just above the manger, Peter the sheep began to sing loudly, “Baaa! Baaaaaa! Baaaa!”

“Be quiet!” shouted the ox, his mouth full of hay.

But all night long Peter sang and sang while everyone else

tried to sleep. Then, just as everyone else seemed to be stirring and waking, Peter decided it was time for a little nap. He curled up on the hay and closed his eyes.

Soon, chatter filled the little stable. Chickens clucked, the donkey brayed, the ox lowed, mice squeaked. Before long it began to sound like one big birthday party. Peter couldn't stand it any longer. He opened his eyes, and when he did, two mice were standing right there in front of him. They said something

about a party, but he ignored them. He even started singing so he wouldn't have to listen to them. "Baaaaa! Baaaaaa!"

He was baaing when he noticed the bright light near the manger. And there was singing—

beautiful singing. It was so much better than anything he'd ever heard that old rooster do. He wondered what was happening over there by the manger.

# Four

# Thomas the Rooster

"It's just not worth it," said Thomas the Rooster to the weasel. He turned one eye to look at the light the man had placed on the shelf. Then he turned his head to look at it with his other eye.

"Tell me about it," said the weasel, who wasn't supposed to be in the stable at all. But he figured that if there was a rooster here, there were probably hens here too. And hens meant there were probably eggs. Ah, delicious eggs.

"You keep your eyes open—both of them—watching for the sun to rise so that you can wake everyone up," grumped the rooster. "Then some man comes in with a lamp bright enough to wake the world. Go figure!"

The weasel scratched his chin and said, more slowly and more weasel-like, "So you've decided not to crow anymore, no matter what happens?"

"Not planning to," Thomas answered.

"What about when the sun comes up?" asked the weasel.

The rooster shook his head, his comb flapping like a wet leaf. "Doubt it. Have to get up too early. I just want to sleep in for once, like the rest of you guys."

The weasel grinned, because he liked what he was hearing. He asked, "What about crowing to scare off intruders—like someone looking for a nice juicy egg for breakfast?" He licked his lips. Then quickly he wiped the grin from his face and said, "Not that I know of anyone like that."

The rooster shook his head again. "Doubt it. Let everyone take care of himself. I'm tired of guard duty. Now, if you'll excuse me, it's time to take a nap—a nice, long nap."

To celebrate his new life of not being a rooster, Thomas flapped up to a wooden beam overhead, tucked his head under one wing to cover his eyes, and fell fast asleep.

He woke up

once when a couple of mice tried

to tell him something about a baby and a

party, but then he went straight back to sleep.

Finally the singing woke him. He pulled his

head from beneath his wing just enough so

that one eyeball was out. It was daylight. He had missed the sun!

He could see two mice dancing on a grain storage jar as if they were having one big party. What in the world was going on? And there, on the beam not far away, was a silly animal swinging by its tail and grinning like an … opossum. Now what was that all about?

# Five

# Zacchaeus the Opossum

"I can hang by my tail," said the opossum. His name was Zacchaeus. He was talking to a donkey that had come in with the man who had brought the light.

“Sounds like that would hurt,” said the donkey.

The opossum shook his head. “Doesn’t hurt at all. I could swing by my tail all night if I had to. And you know what else?”

“What?”

“I can grin.” With that, Zacchaeus the Opossum flashed a big, sparkling smile, showing off dozens of shiny white teeth.

The donkey was impressed and tried to smile too, but when she tried to stretch her big lips into a grin, they flapped back over her teeth and covered up her smile.

"But the best thing of all," said the opossum, "I can play dead better than anyone else. Watch this."

And with that, the opossum flipped over onto his back, stuck all four feet in the air, and looked as dead as dead could be. In fact, he was acting so dead, he was missing all the excitement. The donkey tried to wake him up. A couple of mice tried to wake him up. But the opossum was too good. It wasn't until the donkey began to sing—like everyone else—that the opossum came to.

By now, the stable was a bit crowded, and the opossum thought maybe he'd created the excitement. "It's okay," said the opossum. "It's what I do. I play dead! No need to panic! Show's over."

"I don't think they were watching you," said the donkey.

"Oh? Then what?"

The donkey turned her head in the same direction as the sheep and the ox. She even managed to grin. "They came to see him."

"Him? Who?"

Zacchaeus sat up and stretched as tall as he could, but he didn't even reach as high as the donkey's lower lip. "I can't see!" shouted Zacchaeus. "I can't see!" But there was too much noise for

anyone to hear little Zacchaeus. There was clucking and braying and mooing and squeaking. And was . . . was that . . . a baby crying?

"Hop on my back," said the donkey. "Then you can see."

So Zacchaeus scurried up the donkey's back leg as if it were a tree trunk and sat upon her back. He could see a little better, but if he could only get up to that beam—the one just over the manger—he could see better. He climbed quickly. Then he looped his long tail

around the beam and hung down above the wonderful sight that everyone was looking at and singing about.

From here, he could see everything beautifully. *Wow! This is incredible*, he thought. From here he could even see that trembling little cat that lay shaking beneath the manger.

# Maggie the Cat

There once was a cat named Maggie. Mary Magdalene was her real name, but everyone called her Maggie. Maggie knew it was not going to be a good night the moment the man burst into the stable carrying that light. All she wanted right now was a nice,

quiet, dark place where she could hide and rest. She wanted to hide because she was afraid of everything—noises, people, opossums, and even mice. Maggie, who could swallow a mouse whole if she wanted to, was really nothing more than a big scaredy cat.

She had been lying near a pile of hay, but the mean old ox had shouted at her to move. Now she lay curled up all alone beneath

the manger filled with straw. She was shaking from fright because a mouse had just stopped by and chatted on and on about some big party. Mice were so creepy. If she could just make it 'til morning. Daytime wasn't nearly as scary—except, of course, when that old rooster crowed at dawn. Now that was a scary sound.

But tonight was different because there were more animals in the stable than usual. She wondered what was going on.

Oh, my! What was that noise? What was that sound? A baby crying? Why was there a baby right here in the stable? This place was for animals only.

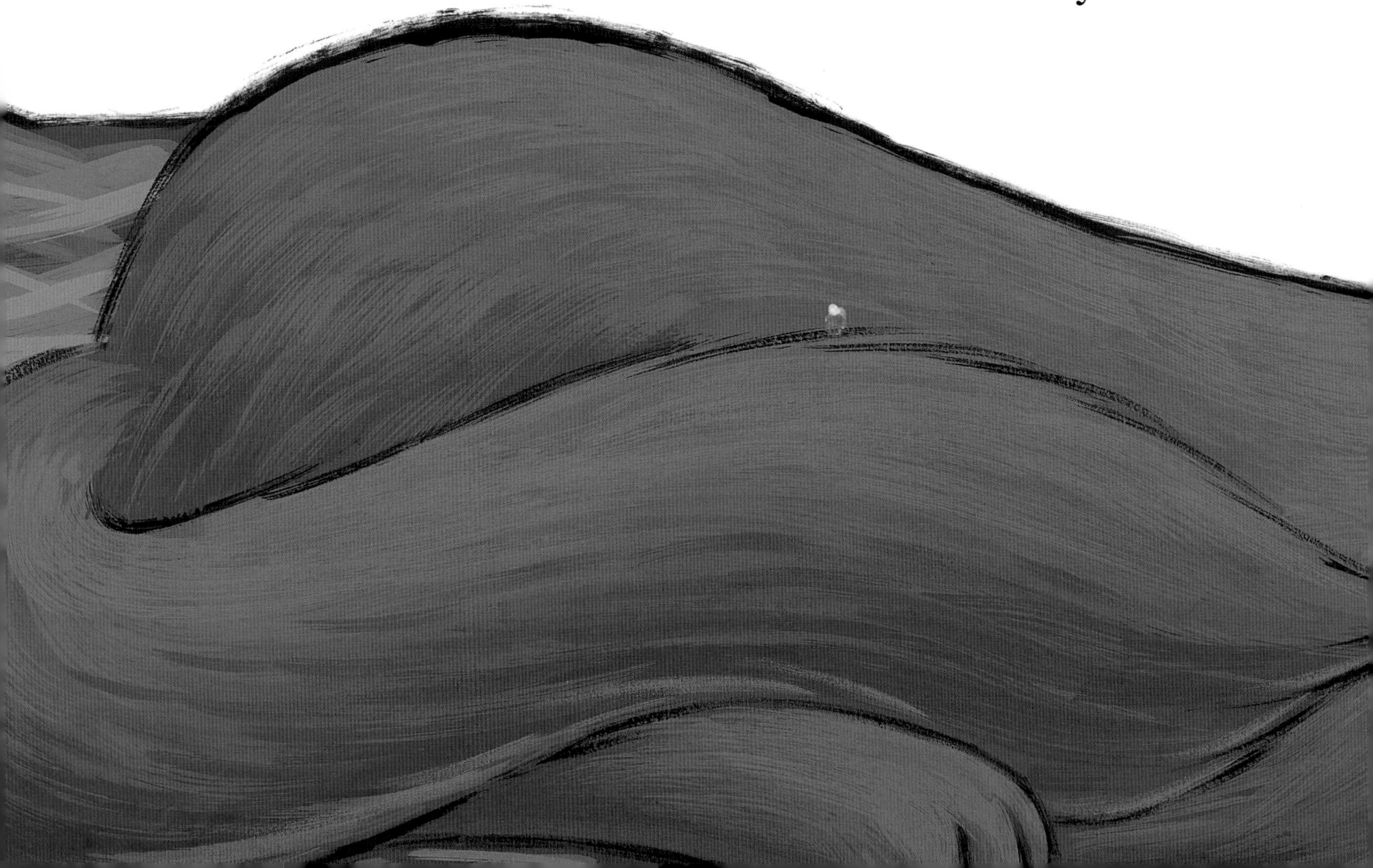

Yet the noise was coming from just above her, from the hay in the manger.

She had to get away. She uncurled just a bit and peeked out over her furry paws. She saw that the room was no longer

dark but very, very bright—and it was even noisier than before. An ox was lowing, a rooster was crowing, a sheep was singing (badly), the mice were squeaking, and above them all, an opossum was swinging by his tail from a wooden beam.

Slowly, she crawled out from beneath the manger, trembling and staying low to the ground. Not far from her was a hole in the wall that led to the outside. If she could just make it out,

she could hide somewhere. In the night there were lots of places to hide, away from the sounds, away from the light. She was nearly to the hole in the wall, when someone—something—grabbed her by the scruff of her neck and lifted her from the ground. It was the man who had set the light on the shelf.

*Oh, my, this is scary, she thought. Oh, my! OH, MY!*

OH . . . MY! What a beautiful sight!

She'd never seen anything like this before. She had never felt like this before. She looked into the manger and suddenly she was not afraid. Not even the squeaky little mice scurrying below could frighten her now.

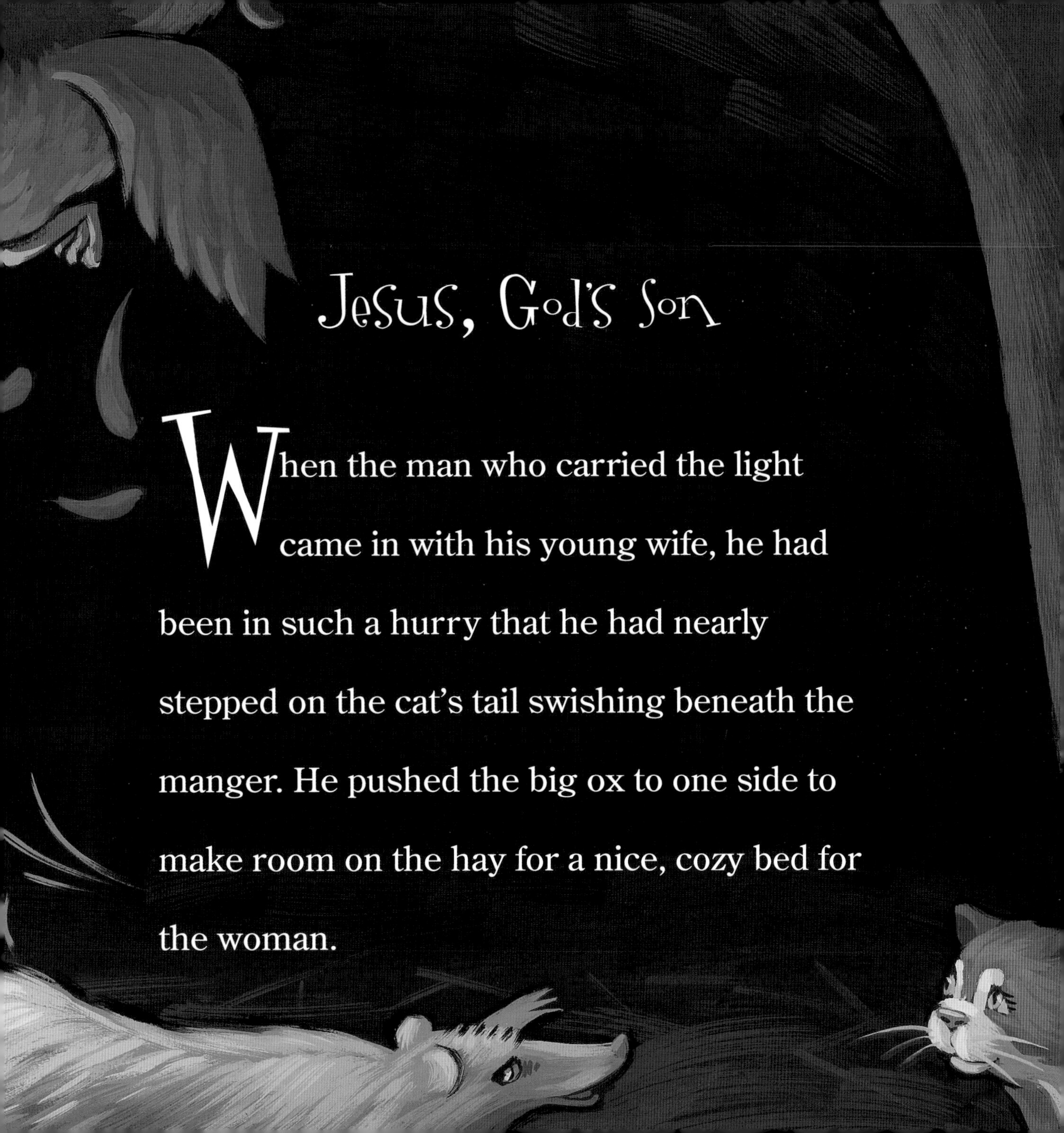

## Jesus, God's Son

When the man who carried the light came in with his young wife, he had been in such a hurry that he had nearly stepped on the cat's tail swishing beneath the manger. He pushed the big ox to one side to make room on the hay for a nice, cozy bed for the woman.

There had been quite a bit of noise in the little stable with all the animals moving around. But all that animal chatter was nothing compared to the sound the little baby boy made when he took his first breath! All the animals hushed (at least for a moment) and listened, and then they began to crowd in closer.

The big ox wasn't too happy about being pushed out of his spot, a spot so close to the manger filled with hay. So he took a step back, and when he did he saw the baby. *Goodness,*

he thought, *so tiny, so helpless, so loud.*

Suddenly, Saul wanted to tell

someone else—

everyone else—about

this. "Hey, Peter!" he

said to the sheep.

"You've got to

see this."

“See what?” said Peter. “And what’s making all that noise?”

“It’s a baby,” said Saul. “Come see.” And the big bully ox politely stepped aside so the sheep could get a better look.

Peter didn’t want to take a look, but he did. “Who is he?”

“He’s the one who made us,” said the big ox.

Peter whipped around. Was that a catch in the ox’s voice? Was Saul crying?

*That baby must be a shepherd,* Peter thought. And right then, he decided he would follow this new little shepherd who lay there on the hay.

And along with the little baby, Peter the Sheep began to sing: "Baaaaa! Baaaaa!"

On a wooden beam overhead hung Zacchaeus the Opossum. He was hanging near a sleeping rooster. He couldn't believe what he was seeing. "He made us?" he said.

Maggie the Cat had thought she was going to die from fright when the man first picked her up. She'd never been held like this before.

But while the man scratched behind her ears, Maggie looked at the baby. Just then the baby stopped crying. Was he smiling? At Maggie?

She purred. She'd never purred before. She'd always been too afraid. The baby moved

his tiny hands, waving them in the air, as if he were pointing to that silly old opossum that dangled and grinned overhead.

Finally, all the noise woke Thomas the Rooster. He pulled

his sleepy head out from under his wing to see that it was daylight. Why, he'd missed the sun! He looked around and saw the ox and the sheep below. They were standing close like friends. A man was holding a cat who was purring loudly. Not far away an opossum swung by his tail, and the two mice he'd heard earlier were jumping up and down as if they were having a grand old party. Then he saw a brand-new baby in the manger. Now where did that come from?

What had been going on? *You try to sleep in one morning and the place goes crazy!* he thought.

But there was something about that baby. The baby seemed to be smiling. He seemed so warm and bright, lying there in the manger. The old rooster had seen lots of sunrises in his time, but nothing ever like this.

"Ox says he made us," said the opossum.

"Ox said that?" asked Thomas.

"Sure did," Saul the Ox answered. "You see, he's God's Son."

Thomas the Rooster got very excited at this news. He knew just what he was supposed to do. From his perch high above the manger, the rooster pulled his head back, and he crowed louder and longer than he had ever crowed before. "COCK-A-DOODLE-DO!"

He was crowing in a brand-new day—the day God's Son came to earth!

Mary and Martha Mouse danced on top of a clay jar. They had invited everyone they knew, and everyone had come to their birthday party for the little baby. And they hadn't even had to decorate. It was the greatest celebration ever!

And it all happened there that night, in a little stable, in a little town called Bethlehem, when God's own Son, Jesus Christ, came to live with those he had created. And that includes you and me.

# And The Story Goes On...

So that's how it was with the animals the night when Jesus was born. Everyone knew there was something special happening that night, and it wasn't because of anything like extra straw, or more animals, or even the glowing lamp on the post. That feeling of something special had everything to do with the little baby named Jesus.

The mice, the opossum, the sheep, the scaredy cat, the rooster, even that old bully ox were all changed that night. They became friendlier, happier, and more helpful.

But the most incredible part of this story is that today the little baby Jesus is still changing lives. Maybe he's even changed your heart.

And that would be the greatest of all the tales from the manger!

Meow! Baa! Squeak! COCK-A-DOODLE-DO! And Merry Christmas!

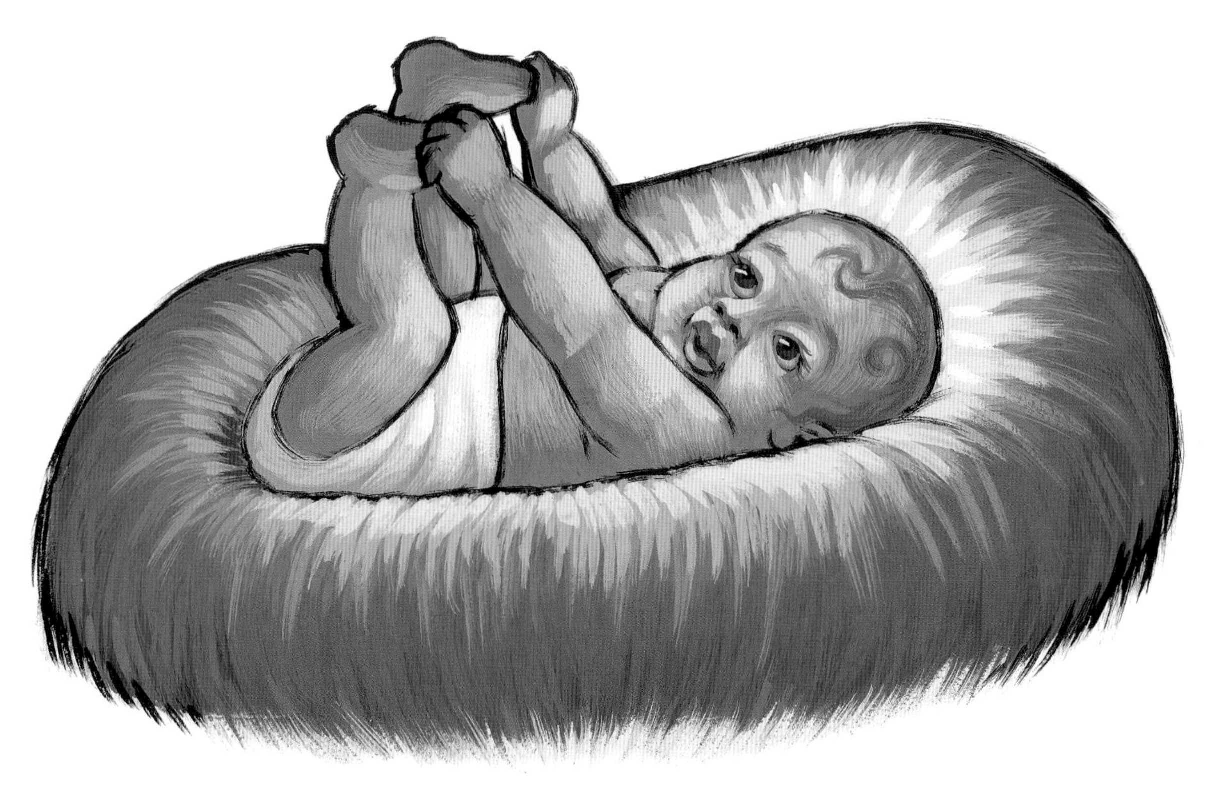

We want to hear from you. Please send your comments about this book to us in care of zreview@zondervan.com. Thank you.

*Grand Rapids, MI 49530*
www.zonderkidz.com